Milkies In The Morning

By Jennifer Saleem

Jennifer Saleem/Jennifer Saleem Books

www.jennifersaleembooks.com

info@jennifersaleembooks.com

Publisher's Note: This is a work of fiction. Names, characters, places, and incidents are a product of the author's imagination. Locales and public names are sometimes used for atmospheric purposes. Any resemblance to actual people, living or dead, or to businesses, companies, events, institutions, or locales is completely coincidental.

Book design © 2013, BookDesignTemplates.com

Ordering Information: Special discounts are available on quantity purchases by corporations, associations, and others. For details, contact the publisher at the web address above.

United States / Jennifer Saleem — First Edition

ISBN 978-0-9854159-5-2

Printed in the United States of America

Dedication

This book is dedicated to my sweet Tiny who started life as a little "Peanut" and took me on a wild breastfeeding journey that lasted over 4 years. Tiny Wonder, Little Love, Babycakes, and Little Little, you grabbed my heart from the first moment I learned you were growing inside me and never let it go. Thank you for always being my most persistent teacher, my muse, and my friend. I love you to the moon, past the sun, and more than all the stars in the sky.

A special thank you to my Moogie. Without your loving guidance, words of encouragement, and nonintrusive support, I would have failed at breastfeeding.

Thoughts from the Author

The subject of weaning is a touchy one at best. For breastfeeding mothers and their nurslings, there is a lot more to breastfeeding than just nourishment. There is the bond, the comfort, the routine.

There does come a time when, for whatever reason, it is time for the mother and child to end the nighttime breastfeeding relationship. Sometimes this happens organically. The child begins to sleep through the night or simply finds other ways to soothe him or herself after waking. Other times, the mother needs to initiate the change in the breastfeeding relationship. This is a lot easier in concept then in reality.

When it was time for me to initiate night weaning with my daughter, it was actually incredibly difficult. Horrible for the both of us to be frank. Neither of us was ready. So I continued on for another 18 months. And then, it was really time to night wean my then almost 4-year-old.

As I sat with myself one day pondering how this would look, it occurred to me that my daughter was always more likely to accept a change if I created a story around it. Hearing the story for several days or weeks in advance of the event almost always made for a seamless transition. And so I thought..."why not write a book?" And I did.

I read this same story to my daughter for two weeks before the big event. By the end of the 6th night, she was asking me if we were going to stop having milkies like the girl in the story. When I told her yes, it was time, she nodded. Another week went by and one night my daughter said "I don't need milkies tonight." And for the first time in 4 years and 4 months, she did not wake for milk.

Just like that, my daughter was night weaned.

I credit the success of our night weaning efforts both to her developmental readiness but also to this story. It made the concept seem more normal, something that she could relate to since "other children were also doing it."

I hope that this book helps ease the transition from night-nursing to night weaning for you and your child no matter his or her age. This book is filled with love, strength, and encouragement from me to you. Let it wrap around you and your child like the warm embrace of an old friend supporting you during a difficult part of your life journey.

Peace and love!

Good night my love
Close your eyes
Have some milk
Then lullabies

With one last kiss and milkies done

Go to sleep my little one

I know it's hard,
I understand
Cuddle up tight
I'll hold your hand

I'll stroke your back and
sing to you
But no more milk
The day is through

You are older and need
more rest

You can't be glued to
mama's breast

You need to sleep
And so do I
Hush my darling
No need to cry

I'll hold you close
All safe and snug
With lots of kisses
And tons of hugs

In the morning
It's milkies for you
They'll still be there
Yes, it's true

The moon is now gone
Here comes the sun
It's milkie time
My little one

Links to websites, articles, resources, and books can also be found at:

http://www.hybridrastamama.com/breastfeeding-links

Resources

Breastfeeding Support Websites

La Leche League International (http://www.llli.org/) - is the #1 source for breastfeeding information. If you are looking for in-person assistance, you may also be able to find La Leche League meetings (http://www.llli.org/search/groups) near you. In person meetings with other breastfeeding mothers can be enormously more valuable than online information, especially if you are new to breastfeeding, having any issues, needing some friendly support, or just want to be in company that understands you. Even if there are no meetings near you, the La Leche League Leaders listed on the meeting pages will all be happy to talk to you on the phone or through email if you need breastfeeding support.

Kelly Mom (http://kellymom.com/) - is a trustworthy site, well organized to address many different issues.

Books

Please visit my Amazon breastfeeding reading list to find and purchase the books noted below plus many more.
http://astore.amazon.com/hybrasmam-20?_encoding=UTF8&node=14

- Adventures in Tandem Nursing
- Breastfeeding Made Simple
- Breastfeeding Older Children
- Dr. Jack Newman's Guide to Breastfeeding
- How Weaning Happens
- Ina May's Guide to Breastfeeding
- Mothering Your Nursing Toddler
- The Nursing Mother's Companion
- The Politics of Breastfeeding
- The Womanly Art of Breastfeeding

Additional Breastfeeding Support Websites

- Ask Dr. Sears (http://www.askdrsears.com/)

- Best for Babes (http://www.bestforbabes.org/)

- Biological Nurturing (http://www.biologicalnurturing.com/)

- Breastfeeding Moms Unite!
  (http://www.breastfeedingmomsunite.com/)

- Breastfeeding Online
  (http://www.breastfeedingonline.com/meds.shtml)

- Breastfeeding USA (https://breastfeedingusa.org/)

- Common Sense Breastfeeding (http://www.normalfed.com/)

- Dr. Hale's Infant Risk Center (http://www.infantrisk.com/)

- Dr. Jack Newman's Breastfeeding Help Handouts
  (http://www.drjacknewman.com/breastfeeding-help.asp)

- Human Milk Banking Association of North America
  (https://www.hmbana.org/)

- Human Milk 4 Human Babies (http://www.hm4hb.net/)

- If Breastfeeding Offends You Put A Blanket Over Your Head
  (http://www.facebook.com/pages/If-breastfeeding-offends-you-put-a-
  blanket-over-YOUR-head/444758635156?ref=pb)

- International Breastfeeding Center (http://www.nbci.ca/index.php?option=com_content&view=frontpage&Itemid=1)
- International Lactation Consultant Association (http://www.ilca.org/i4a/pages/index.cfm?pageid=1)
- Kangaroo Mother Care (http://www.kangaroomothercare.com/)
- Low Milk Supply (http://www.lowmilksupply.org/)
- Medications and Mother's Milk (http://www.medsmilk.com/)
- National Milk Bank (http://www.nationalmilkbank.org/)
- Natural Mother Magazine (http://www.naturalmothermagazine)
- Natural Parents Network (http://www.naturalparentsnetwork.com)
- Normalizing Nursing In Public League (http://www.facebook.com/NNIPL?ref=pb)
- Nursing Freedom (http://www.nursingfreedom.org/)
- The Lactation Consultant Directory (http://www.breastfeeding.com/directory/lcdirectory.html)
- The Leaky Boob (http://www.facebook.com/TheLeakyBoob?ref=pb)

- United States Breastfeeding Committee (http://www.usbreastfeeding.org/Home/tabid/36/Default.aspx)
- Work and Pump (http://www.workandpump.com/)
- World Alliance For Breastfeeding Action (http://www.waba.org.my/)
- World Health Organization Growth Charts for Breastfed Babies (http://www.who.int/childgrowth/standards/chart_catalogue/en/index.html)

About the Author

A little about me... I am the author of **Hybrid Rasta Mama**, a blog sharing my views, experience, insights and research on any and all things related to conscious parenting, natural/mindful living, holistic health/wellness, real food and much more. My goal is to inspire people around the world to take what I have researched and written, do further research if needed, and apply it to their families and their lives.

I am also the co-organizer of the **Healthy Child Summit**, an audio conference educating, inspiring, and empowering parents to care for their families naturally.

Where Else Can You Find Me?

- Visit my blog (http://www.hybridrastamama.com)
- Subscribe to the Hybrid Rasta Mama Newsletter (http://www.hybridrastamama.com/p/subscribe-to-my-newsletter.html)
- Check out my other breastfeeding children's books, real food recipes, and health books (http://www.jennifersaleembooks.com)
- Like Hybrid Rasta Mama on Facebook (http://www.facebook.com/HybridRastaMama)
- Follow Hybrid Rasta Mama on Twitter (http://twitter.com/hybridrastamama)
- Follow Hybrid Rasta Mama on Pinterest (http://pinterest.com/hybridrastamama/)
- Learn more about the Healthy Child Summit (http://www.hybridrastamama/healthy-child-summit)

Lightning Source UK Ltd.
Milton Keynes UK
UKRC01n0717121016
285062UK00003B/6